Lil' Boot

Some Kind of a Hero

Margo Cunningham

Happy Reading!

Margo Cunningham

"One can never have too many cats."
Glenara Dalzen

Dedication

Dedicated to my grandchildren, Bailey and Chris, in memory of their cat, Lil' Boot.

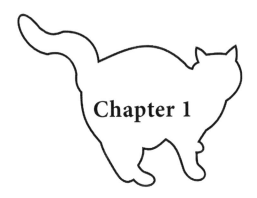

Chapter 1

How it Began

"Meow, Meow, Meow," pitiful cries come from my brothers and sisters. Baby, the runt of the litter, has been mewing sadly since we were packed up so suddenly. Smokie, Thomas, and Greybee are tumbling over each other trying to play, trying to get out.

"Ouch! Get off my tail!" I grouse at them. "There isn't enough room in this cage for you three to be messing around, so stop!" As I give them each a good thump on their heads, they seem to calm down.

"Mom! Mom! Little Boot just bopped us on the head!"

No reply. Mom is lying on her side, panting, eyes wide, and peering straight ahead. This scares us more than anything. Oh, she was brave and tried to comfort us as our world fell apart, but once the truck pulled out of town she has been mute.

It had begun as a beautiful day. The grass in the clearing was waving gently. The birds were singing. The bugs and mice were a plenty. We were enjoying the sunshine and mom was teaching us to hunt. "Mom, Greybee's eating all of the mouse's tails," I grumbled.

"Hush, Lil' Boot, you'll get your share." She giggles at me. "You always do."

FLUMP!!! A huge net swoops over us. Screaming and dashing in every direction, we try to run; but it is no use. We are scooped up and rudely tossed into a wire cage. We had been so busy eating and enjoying ourselves that we didn't hear the man creeping up on us. Crash! The cage is flung into the back of a truck.

"Got ya! Got ya, momma cat and your

scruffy, miserable kittens. Now, we are off to my secret facility in Mexico. Moore, Montana will be short six cats, but no loss. My dream is to rid the country of cats. Thanks to you all, I'm one step closer to my dream."

"Ha, momma cat! You and your brood didn't have a chance. I've been watching you for days. They don't call me the **Boogey Man** for nothing. I always get what I want. Now, your worst nightmare is about to begin."

The truck began to move slowly at first but then it gathered speed. We huddled together as the horrifying journey commenced. The motion is frightening and Thomas is feeling sick.

"At least we are together," Momma cooed. "Baby, I know you don't like the dark, but those dirty windows in the doors give us some light." Momma gives Baby a comfort bath.

"Momma, where are they taking us?" shivered Greybee softly.

"I don't know," sighed Momma. "Listen, Boot, I'm going to need your help with the young ones. You like to explore and toy with things, please try to get us out of here."

"Yes, momma," I reply, but I think to myself, *I'm scared, too!*

Looking around I see dirty metal walls and two very well locked doors. Mom is right; the windows are small and smudged with layers of crud.

"Cripes!" This darn latch doesn't want to budge. How am I going to open the door? Before I can make any headway the truck slows to a stop. We are shaking, crying, and overcome with fear. What now?

We silently wait in the darkness. Time seems to have stopped. It seems that the men have left us. I try to bat the latch. Heavy footsteps approach the truck. Loud voices are grumbling at each other.

"Get the door!"

Thunk! Clank! Woosh! As the doors are flung open, the light is blinding. The men appear as looming shadows and toss another cage into the truck.

"Mew, mew," pitiful whimpering is coming from the new addition. "What, what is going on?" a weak voice asks us.

"I'm afraid that you are not going to like the answer," Mom gently replies.

"My name is Morris," a big orange tom answers.

"My name is Samantha," a small white cat adds. "We've been traveling together for some time. This was not part of our plans."

Mom introduces us to our new traveling companions and starts to tell our tale. "We were enjoying the day; the kittens were trying their paws at hunting when… when"… sob.

"Mom, I'll finish," I sigh. In the murky gloom I can feel Morris and Samantha shrink into each other with fear as I explain about the Boogey Man and his evil plans.

The truck is moving again. As frightful as this is, the stopping is worse. Each stop means that the Boogey Man is deadly serious to carry out his plan. After travelling for what seems like forever, the truck slows to a stop. The men leave.

"Morris," I whisper, "try batting your latch. I plan to get us out of here when we stop and you two should come with us." He began to worry his latch.

Once again the angry voices return to the truck and the doors are flung open. Thump! Thwap! Two more cages were tossed into the truck.

"Yowl!" screams a big Siamese cat. "You just wait until my owners get a hold of you, buster! &#@%*$^! What are you looking at?" he sneers at us.

"Rudeness and threats won't get you out of here," quips my mom. "Be quiet and settle down. You're upsetting my kittens."

"Well, excuse me!!! Tell me what is going on."

"I'll handle this, Momma." I introduce Morris, Samantha, and the rest of us. Before I go into our tale and all of our fate, I want to know the names of the three cats in the second cage. They are Panther, Purrcy, and Suki.

After I finish our tale of woe and the dismal fate awaiting all of us, the Siamese bellows, "NO! No way, not going to happen to me!" He turns his back to us and begins to pout. A low grumbling comes from his cage.

Moving, stopping, moving, stopping; the pattern lasts for days. Oh, the men did feed us, but they never let us out. Let me tell you that being stuck in a cage with five other cats and a fowl kitty pan is disgusting. Ew, the stench was becoming unbearable.

Rattle, Rattle, Bang! Our cage slides

around the back of the old truck banging into other cages and rattling with every bump. It was worse before the other cages were added, then we were thrown hither and yon. There has to be over twenty cages filled with cats. Cats of all shapes and sizes and each one complaining loudly. Crying and crying, they are crying for their lost home, their lost families, and their lost freedom. Such a cruel fate. The din is giving me a headache.

If only momma wasn't so quiet, I could be brave. Being the first born, I'm bigger than the rest of my littermates. I've always been the first to try things. I opened my eyes first. I was the first to crawl. The first to catch a spider.

None of the other kittens are orange like me. We all are different colors. I'm long and lean and striped from head to toe. It looks almost like an "M" on my forehead. Momma says, "It's because I am always thinking me, me, me." But I know that the M means mighty. Yes, that's right, Mighty Boots.

"Get off, Smokie! It's too hot to having you climbing on me," I grumble.

He replies sheepishly, "Yeah, have you noticed that it's been getting warmer and warmer? I'm so bored. We've been going forever and ever."

"What is Mexico?" Greybee whines.

Nobody seems to know. Every time another cage is added we ask them. We now have cages from Montana, Wyoming, Colorado, and New Mexico. The last cages were added in some place called Las Cruces, New Mexico.

They tell us that Mexico is a very hot, dry country south of the United States. It is home to snakes and scorpions, not a place for kitties. We just have to cross the Rio Grande River to be there. This news is too much for our young kitten brains to take. Baby is crying; Smokie, Thomas, and Greybee are rolling around; and Momma is staring and panting.

I'm thinking, *Something has to be done. I'm not going!* I've been watching the latch on our cage. Every bump seems to move the latch a little. If I can stretch up as long as I can, I will bat it with my paw. When I scrunch my eyes it looks like a shiny worm. Bat-bat-bat-it starts to swing.

Crash! Rumble! Bang! Screech! Wump, wump, wump! The truck has hit a hole and blew a tire. The cages are falling, slipping, crashing, and flying everywhere. We are bounced around and flung into each other. With a loud crunch our cage hits the floor and the door springs open.

The noise is deafening! A hundred cats are hissing and screaming. Other cats have started batting their latches, so there are cats loose and scared. It is pandemonium. Cats are leaping and running, growling and hissing, banging into each other and in a panic.

A loud chain of curses comes from the front of the truck. "Louie, Phil move to the side of the road and grab the nets. We've got cats trying to make a break. Hurry up, you idiots! If even one cat gets away, I'll have your heads!" The Boogey Man roars.

"Momma, momma, move! Get Baby and be ready to run. Smokie, Thomas, Greybee, follow me!" We move together towards the door. A huge Siamese cat stands between us and freedom.

"I'm going first, runt. Keep your family out of the way," he growls.

Whoosh! The door swings open and the Siamese charges the light. Oh no, the men are there with nets. The next moment everything goes crazy. Cats are running every which way and everywhere screaming as they go. The men are yelling and the nets are swishing. The noise is deafening. Bigger cats keep pushing past us.

"Momma, we have to go now!" I scream.

With a powerful shove Momma and Baby are moving. Smokie, Thomas, and Greybee are hot on my tail. Two black cats leap smack in front of us causing Momma and Baby to slide into the door and are trapped there by one of the men. Poor Momma and Baby are caught.

"No!" I scream as I jump over the man. Thud, roll, and then splash! I hate water! Where are Smokie, Thomas, and Greybee? They should be landing on me by now.

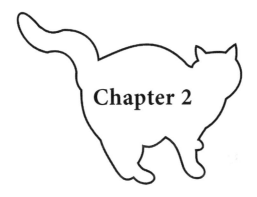

Chapter 2

Something Lost and Something Gained

Hack, hack, my mouth is filled with dirty water. Gasping, I wildly fling my paws around trying to reach the bank. Silently I plead, "Just let me reach the shore." I don't care that I'm doing the dog paddle; I just have to make it.

As I drag myself onto the rocks, something feels very wrong. There is slimy, green goo everywhere. My paws, belly, and tail are covered in the stinking stuff. Weakly, I drag myself out of the mess. Only two more steps and I'm out of it. I stumble and fall behind a bush.

"It looks like my minions have missed one. Yuk, orange and green, slimy with goo. Maybe, I should leave you here to die? Here, kitty, kitty."

"Hiss! Spit!"

"Hiss and spit all you want, you flea bitten, bum. You're still going to my lab. The world will be free of cats, but not soon enough. You thought you could escape the Boogey Man, but nobody does."

The goo makes my skin crawl. The Boogey Man's evil sneer triggers a panic attack in me. My fur puffs, a growl leaves my throat, and I lunge towards him.

Taken by surprise he falls backwards with me following him down. My claws slash at his face and he tries to roll away. My panic erupts with a burst of fur from me. Shaking and hissing I scratch my way over him and run.

A-a-a-choooo! Cough! Snort! Sputter! Sounds of distress follow my retreat. Seems like the Boogey Man is allergic to cats. I run as if the devil is on my tail. Fear pushes me on. I run. My mind is gone and all I can do is run. When I collapse there is no river, no truck, and no road. "Where am I?" I drag myself into a culvert and faint.

Much later I try to open my eyes and try to stand, but I'm too weak. Wherever the goo has touched my skin is burnt. My muscles ache and I realize that I am alone. "Woe is me! I'm alone and miserable." Tears streak my face. Slowly my tongue moves to my paws. It is such an ugly taste. My tongue throbs, but I must get it off. My throat seems to contract as the goo burns down it and I pass out. How many times, I don't know.

"Señor! Señor!"

"Eh?" I thought. "What?"

"Señor, wake up. You don't look so good. Are you ok?" The voice is like nothing I had ever heard before. It is high pitched and squeaky.

"Where am I?" I sputter. My eyes slowly open. "No way – it can't be." There is a very big mouse and he is speaking to me.

"Hola, Señor."

"Who are you?" I choke at the strange mouse. He is big, I mean huge for a mouse. He is wearing a cape and a mustache. My voice sounds like a hoarse bullfrog.

"Aqua?" he offers. As I drink he tells me his story.

"My name is Archibald Magnanimous Sanchez, the third and last of the *Amazing Mouse Troupe* from Spain. We performed in circuses all over the world. Sí, my five brothers and I could fly on the trapeze, nimbly tread the high wire, and tumble with the best of them. Our skill and daring left audiences gasping and speechless. Kings and queens wanted to see us perform. But, alas there was a freak accident aboard a luxury cruise liner on our way to the U.S."

"Oh, what sorrow – such a cruel fate! All because…No, I can't bear to tell you the details, but I'm the only one left. I survived because of cunning and my daring skills as a circus performer. Plus, more luck than my brothers."

"Since then I have been traveling the country helping the less fortunate and protecting the weak. They call me Macho Mouse. You can call me Mouse"

"Mouse, I am afraid that my story is as sad as yours." As I tell him my story we both begin to sniffle and sob.

"Such sorrow, my friend," he offers. "Perhaps, we can travel together?"

What to do? Do I try to find my momma and the family? Do I go to stop the Boogey Man from stealing cats? Mouse has heard of the Boogey Man. He doesn't think that we should go to Mexico right now. The Boogey Man is a National Hero there and well thought of too. Perhaps later when I am stronger, I will save them.

Silently I pledge, "Momma, be strong! Smokie, Thomas, Greybee, and Baby need you to be strong. I will come for you!" I vow.

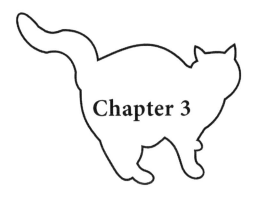

Chapter 3

A Strange Encounter

The heat in Texas sucks the energy plumb out of you. Mouse seems to take it better than me. We've been traveling by night not only because it is cooler, but it is also safer. It seems like the Boogey Man has spies everywhere. We just barely escaped from the last rest stop in New Mexico before you enter Texas.

"Aw, look! Those poor little guys are

stuck on a leaf in the middle of that puddle. I'm going to push the leaf over to safety." Mouse whispers over his shoulder.

"OK, Mouse, but... but, I think that Ranger over there is watching us."

For all of his strength, Macho Mouse can be so gentle and he has a heart of gold. We have helped so many critters in the short time that we have been together. Why there have been at least four mice, a gopher or two and a snake; plus that covey of quail.

"Yes, she is definitely watching us!" The Ranger made a phone call and is now creeping towards us.

"There you go little friends," beams Macho Mouse.

"Mouse, move, NOW! The Ranger is almost on us."

As she lunges towards us, we bound into the brush. We scurry further and further into the brambles. Thunderous footsteps come crushing after us. Mouse puts on the steam and we jet away into a nearby gully.

"Drat! Where did those two get off to? I better call the Boogey Man to let him know that I lost the cat. Lucky for me the Boogey Man is already in Mexico," laments the

Ranger.

"Wait, Mouse!" Pant! Gasp! "I can't run any further. We've covered enough ground for now. I can't even see the glow from the rest stop," I pant.

As we flop onto the ground and cuddle close for warmth, my mind hears the Ranger's word, "The Boogey Man is in Mexico." Before I slip into an exhausted state I whimper, "Oh, Momma, please be ok."

"Can you believe all of the lights?" I gasp. El Paso spreads out before us and there are miles and miles of lights. I'm just a country guy from Montana. Never had I seen so many lights and so many people. No way was I going to follow Mouse into that.

Roar! Honk! Screech! The traffic is terrifying. How can two smallish animals make it into the city and survive? (Note to reader, you never call Macho Mouse small.)

As Mouse is telling me the wonders of El Paso, I hear voices behind us.

"I get the big one," snarls a gravely voice.

"No way, I saw them first. You wouldn't of even known they were there, If I hadn't told you," whines a second voice.

"Yeah, so what? I get the big one," the first voice demands.

"Shut up! They're going to hear us. Remember the last time your big mouth scared our dinner away?" snipes the second voice.

"I still get the big one," growls the first voice.

I grab Mouse and leap onto the nearest Vitex bush. Guess fear gave me a rush, 'cuz we land near the top. Two coyotes are starring up in wonder.

"What the... I thought it was two cats, not birds," yaps one of the coyotes.

"I am a cat. My name is Lil' Boot and this here is my friend, Macho Mouse."

"How come we can understand you and you can understand us! How did you get up there?" questions the first coyote.

"I'm not sure that I know the answer to either question. I got thrown into some toxic goo and have been feeling strange every since. Maybe I changed somehow," I share.

"Why don't you come down and be friendly? We could talk better if we were closer," leers the second coyote.

"That may be, but you want to eat us," I

spit back at them.

"No, way!" they both insist.

"You forget, I can understand you and I heard what you were saying as you were sneaking up on us. Besides, there is a reason my friend is called Macho Mouse. And you saw how far I could jump. Maybe I can fight pretty mean, too."

"Oh, Frank, let's give it up? I say we go find some easier prey."

"It's a pity, Bubba! I was in the mood for a juicy cat. That mouse does look a bit wiry, though."

As Bubba and Frank slink off down the draw, I hear them muttering and fighting.

"Shut up, Bubba! Just shut up," Frank laments.

Mouse and I stare at each other and then the stumbling, bumbling coyotes and burst into laughter. "Ha, ha, ha!" Mouse chortles and nearly falls from the bush.

"Stay with me!" I chuckle as I grab him. "Say, we do make a good team; though not in the way we thought we would. Let's hope that if we meet any more bad guys, they'll be as dumb as those two coyotes."

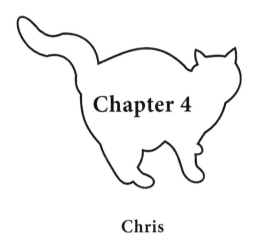

Chris

Chris has a problem. His parents won't listen to him. Worse still, he is in time-out in his room with no computer or video games; no electronics, period.

Drat! Who would have thought they'd get so mad. It wasn't his fault that everything in the closet came crushing down or that the clutter would knock over the table spilling the milk and cereal he had set on the table. How was he to know that pulling out one little, bitty box of Legos would cause such a mess. Arguing with his parents had added to his punishment.

If only his parents would let him have a pet. He just knew he wouldn't get so bored or be in so much trouble all of the time. If only he could get Bailey to talk to them. Bailey was his older sister. Princess Bailey could do no wrong. She seemed to have their parents wrapped around her little finger. Why wouldn't her highness help his cause? He would have to think of some way to make her think *she* wanted a pet.

The more Chris thinks about how unfair it all is, the madder he gets. *I'll show them*, he thinks. The noise from the TV in his parent's bedroom is plenty loud and his sister, Bailey is with them. "I will just sneak away – see if they miss me," fumes Chris.

His bedroom door opens without a sound. Thank goodness for carpeting. The front door is open. Chris carefully opens the screen door and closes it quietly.

Free! I'm free! he thinks as he does a quick victory dance. Without thinking about where he is going, he begins to jog. "When I am bigger," he shouts, "Nobody is going to boss me around!"

Chris is so lost in thought that he traveled quite a distance before he realizes that he doesn't know where he is. He is just about to turn back in the direction of home when he notices a small bridge over an irrigation ditch. Sitting on the bridge is an orange cat who appears to be watching the water.

I wonder if he has a home. Maybe I will just give him a pat or two. I bet a cat would listen to me. "Here, Kitty, Kitty."

The cat slowly turns his head towards Chris and stares with unblinking eyes. He seems to be studying the boy, weighing something in his head.

"I won't hurt you, Kitty! I just want to be your friend," Chris purrs gently to the cat.

The cat doesn't run. Chris slowly moves towards the cat. He wishes he had something to feed the cat. Chris stops close to the cat and bends down to scratch the cat's head.

"Purr – purr – purr!"

The cat seems to want a friend as much as Chris does. "Do you want to come home with me?" Chris gently asks the cat.

"Meow" The cat jumps off the bridge and starts walking in the direction Chris had come from.

"Wait a minute, you, don't know where I live. Let me lead you. Yes, we will stop for pets," laughs Chris.

"Chris, oh Chris!" He could hear his parents calling his name from two blocks away from his home.

"Come on cat, we need to hurry," Chris calls breaking into a trot.

"Meow," says the cat.

His parents see him walking towards them. They cannot believe their eyes. There was their boy and he was walking with a cat. They seem to be talking to each other.

"Boy, what are you doing? You are in big trouble! Don't you ever go off without telling us!" It was hard to tell who was madder, mom or dad.

In the midst of them yelling at him, Chris calmly asks, "Can I keep him?"

Cindy and Ruben stop short. First, they look at each other. Then they look at the boy. Lastly, they look at the cat. True, the boy was in trouble. True, he had been asking for a pet. Plus, the cat seems to want to go home with them.

"Where did you find him?" asks his dad, Ruben.

"Is he someone's pet?" queries his mom, Cindy.

"Are you going to take care of him?" gruffly asks his dad.

"We will let him stay tonight, but we will have to see if we can find his owners tomorrow; before we agree to keep him," his mom adds.

The cat allows Chris to scoop him up and charge for home.

Later in Chris's bedroom the cat is laying on the bed. Chris is beside him slowly stroking the cat's fur. "I wonder what to call you, Chris mummers to the cat."

"I am called Lil' Boot," the cat replies.

"Whoa!" Chris leaps off the bed and gapes at the cat. "Did you just talk to me?"

Lil' Boot blinks, yawns, and says, "Yeah, so …"

"No Way!!! Cats don't … don't talk to people." After thumping his forehead and pinching his arm twice, Chris looks into Lil' Boot's eyes and the cat seems to be amused.

"Take a big breath and sit down. This may take awhile to explain," sighs Lil' Boot.

"Hey, no TV or video games!" exclaims Bailey as she crushes into the room. "I heard voices – what's going on?"

"I was just telling Chris my story when you barged in," mummers Lil' Boot.

"What? You're talking?" Bailey gasps.

"Well, yes. Let me share my story with you. I was getting to the part of how Macho Mouse and I got separated," Lil' Boot explains.

"No way! You are making that up. Wait, you are a talking cat! I guess it could be true." Bailey scratches her head and sinks to the floor.

"Bailey, you just wouldn't believe all of the stuff Lil' Boot has been through," gushes Chris. "He's lost his family and been in toxic goo."

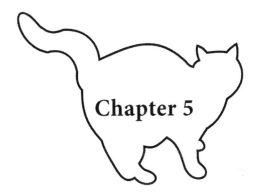

Chapter 5

Losing a Friend

"Hump hum! Let me get on with my story of how I got separated from my friend, Macho Mouse, and ended on the irrigation bridge."

After the scare with the park ranger, my frazzled brain drops me into a deep sleep. Frantic chirping wakes me. There on an ochetto bush is a momma bird calling her chicks. They had been learning to fly, but seemed too weary to get back up to mom. They were running helter-skelter and crashing into each other. In the distance is the sound of thunder and it sounds like it is coming our way.

The Momma bird really freaks when she sees me. "Hold on, Ma'am," I softly try to explain, "We will help you."

Gently, Mouse and I carefully herd the flighty little bird brains out of the arroyo. This was not an easy task and took much longer than we thought it would. Mouse wanted to get them to higher ground before the rain came.

Sure enough the drops start to pummel us. Within minutes everything is drenched and we hear a loud roaring coming towards us.

Out of the corner of my eye I see a desert box turtle trudging up the far bank. As I turn my head to get a better look at him, I see a wall of water flashing down the arroyo.

"Mouse!" I scream as I sprint towards the turtle.

"Here, fellow, let me give you a hand," I say as I scoop him up with my paws and fling him to safety. I barely have time to scamper up next to him. Just to be safe, I give him another bump further up the rise.

Crashing and smashing the water roars

past. It is such a monstrous wall of water that I can't see Mouse or the birds.

I am ashamed to say it, but another panic attack strikes me and I run. I run until I can't run any more. This time I find myself in farming territory. It sure doesn't look like anything they grow in Montana and it is mighty hot; too hot for this old boy.

My heart is heavy. First, I lost momma and my litter mates. Now, I've lost my friend, Macho Mouse. It is all I can do to drag myself up. Where am I? What should I do?

Overcome with grief, I stumble around until I find myself on a small bridge over an irrigation canal. As I stare at my reflection, I am thinking that I must be the world's biggest loser. That is why I was looking at you like I did, Chris. I needed a friend, for sure, but would I let you down, too?

"No, no, no. You saved me from getting a royal thumping from my parents," Chris tells the cat as he is petting him. "You are not a loser, you rescued me."

"We will always love you and take care of you," adds Bailey as she rubs his ears and chin.

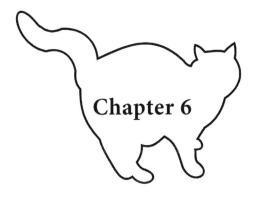

Chapter 6

Bailey

Now Chris is a boy and boys will be boys, and so am I. I am one lean machine, but every once in a while even heroes need a little TLC. Bailey is the person to go to for that.

She has this waterbed that can be so toasty. I admit that it moves a little and I worry about my claws making holes. So when she lies on her back, it is hard to resist stretching out on top of her.

If I tuck my head under her chin and give her licky kisses, I get a warm tingling feeling. When I close my eyes it feels like I am back with mom and I purr.

Being a cat I could stay like this for hours. Before I know it, I have fallen asleep. Bailey, being a human girl, has things to do, people to see or text, and places to go.

"Bootsie! You gotta move," Bailey gently whispers in my ear. "I've got homework to do and I want to call Azalea."

"Umph!" I grump as Bailey gently slides me off of her and onto the covers.

Now, I am not very fond of the nickname, Bootsie, but I'm feeling so very relaxed, and I know that she will be back for more. She loves me too much to keep away from my cuddles for very long.

"More," I mummer through closed lids. She has trouble resisting my strong will, my smiley face, and my sweet purrs.

"Oh, Bootsie Boy. You know I will be back," Bailey adds as she leaves her room. Off she goes to her study area with her cell phone in hand.

Even though I knew she'd be back, I couldn't help but be a little frustrated. There is only one thing that helps this Kitty guy unwind.

What luck! The first bathroom that I come to has a roll of toilet paper just waiting to be shredded. After my practice with cage latches separating toilet paper from the holder is a piece of cake.

To keep my skills sharp, I crouch and leap. As I am flying through the air the toilet paper turns into a vicious rattle snake that needs to be shredded. Claws out, teeth barred, I grab the evil beast by the throat and start clawing with my bucking feet on his scaly belly. What a battle! By the time I'm done with him, he's in a million pieces strewn across the floor. Bailey would be so proud.

Now you would think that my family would be pleased with how I protected them from a nasty varmint, but NO. Cindy shrieks when she sees the toilet paper carnage.

I am exhausted, so I find a comfy secluded place to take a siesta.

Bailey and Chris have been sworn to secrecy concerning my ability to talk. They have done a good job of keeping my secret. We have to be careful around the adults and not talk. I have taught them a code to use.

They listen to my pitch and volume and how many meows I use. Bailey adores me, so she was quick to learn.

"MEOWER-UP, mew, mew," means we need to talk now. Bailey follows me into her room and we close the door. I tell her how much I miss my mom and she scoops me up. I am a bit sad after the scene with Cindy. After some moments of cooing and sweet talk, I ask her about Azalea and her other friends. She loves sharing her secrets with me. We can go on for hours like this.

I like to help Bailey with her homework, but she is one smart puppy and doesn't need much help. I have to content myself with sitting on the table watching her work. Boy, that wiggly pencil looks just like a wounded bug. Bat. Bat.

"Bootsie, you are going to have to move or stop that." She complains.

Drat, she is cute when I bug her. Bat. Bat.

Well, here I am on the floor, swished off of the desk. I hate it when Bailey does that. *What to do, what to do?* I wonder to myself.

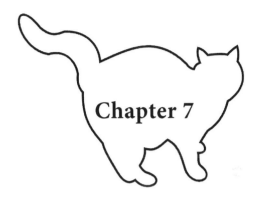

Chapter 7

Life with the Gomez Family

Life is good with the Gomez family. It seems like humans are fairly easy to train. Of course Ruben takes extra work, but he is getting better. I could really get use to being a pampered cat, but I know that sometime soon, I have to rescue Momma.

Just a meow or two can get me what I need. I guess the goo did something to my voice. The humans always laugh at me and say that I have a little girly meow. You would think that Bailey and Chris would cut me some slack, since they know my sad tale of woe, but no, they are human kids and easily amused.

Occasionally, I have to help Cindy remember to feed me. Wump! I use both paws to bat her on the bottom. You should have seen her face the first time I did it. A few of those bats from me and she got the message. Now, I'm her sweet pawtootie. She keeps me fed and quite spoiled.

Of course, my experience with the latches on our cage in the Boogey Man's truck has come in very handy, very handy, indeed. Any cabinet, drawer, or door with a handle is no match for a smart cat like me. The house and everything in it are mine to explore, mine to play with, or mine to eat. A cat could get use to this life.

I should have known that good things never last, but I didn't expect it to end so soon. Can you believe that the family got another cat, Lily? I mean, really, I was all they needed. I provide entertainment and comfort. I give them tasks to do and meaning to their lives. Paws down, I am their best friend.

Lily is all right as cats go. We just don't

seem to think alike and have different interests. She doesn't like that I am number one. Thank goodness she doesn't give licky kisses under people's chins. She's not into talking much to the likes of me. She is so aloof.

I have to share everything with her, the food bowl, the laps, and even the kitty pan. Gross! I'm having a hard time convincing her that I am the boss. She can be fairly stubborn. I get to the food first and to the best laps first. We both go outside to avoid the bathroom problem.

To make matters worse, there has been talk around the house lately, about getting a puppy. Can you believe it, a puppy? Oh yeah, they have been, also, talking about something called a guinea pig. What on earth is a guinea pig? It all just boggles my mind.

Actually, I think that getting more pets will make my leaving easier. We are very close to Mexico here. The Rio Grande is very low, so a cat could find his way across it without getting too wet.

I decide to start exploring the area around our house. There must be a way to get to

Mexico somewhere out there. Every evening I explore a little further.

One night I think I hear my name being called, but I can't figure out which direction it came from. It is not any of my humans. The voice seems familiar, high pitched, but full. This voice haunts my memory.

The family did get a guinea pig. It's a rodent! He is a hungry, selfish animal that lives in a cage. They named him Scooby Doo. Plus, he is not the sharpest crayon in the box. All he does is squeak and squall. He doesn't try to talk to me or Lily and he raises a big stink if we get to close too his cage. If he sees a person, he is begging for food. No dignity at all. At least a cat can charm a person into feeding it.

After my time with Macho Mouse, I had hoped to have a friend like him to talk to about life and other issues. Scooby Doo is definitely not going to be that kind of friend. I don't really care if the humans have carrots.

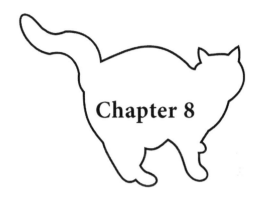

Chapter 8

A Joyous Reunion

One night as I work my way further away from our house, I hear that voice again and it is coming from the other side of a rise. As I move carefully towards it, the reality of who it is dawns on me. Yes, it's my lost friend Macho Mouse.

We race towards each other. He jumps on my face and squeezes with all of his might. "Boot! Boot! Boot! I have found you," gushes Macho Mouse.

"Oh, Mouse, I'm so glad you did!" I happily reply.

Looking me over he says, "Why, you look like one pampered, fat cat. What is this?" he says as he pats my tummy. "Have you gained weight?"

"Maybe." I grudgingly admit. "I found this human family that needed a pet and I just forgot myself."

"But now, you are back?" Mouse gingerly asks.

"Yes, I guess I am." The family has gotten other pets to care for them. They will be ok. I have forgotten about Momma and my quest to find her and my family for way too long.

"You know, Mouse, I have wasted a lot of time. What say, we get started tonight?"

"Si, Senor, I've been waiting to hear those words."

We hadn't gone very far when we approached the Rio Grande River. From the top of the bank it seems very shallow, easy to cross. Mouse leads the way as we carefully clamor towards the bank.

The river bottom is laced with pockets of putrid, dark water. If there isn't a dying fish in the puddle, it is loaded with gooey, black sludge. We decided that we didn't want to know what was in the sludge.

As we carefully approach the small channel of water, Mouse clearly does not like the idea of swimming across it. I have never seen him so nervous. I can see his quivering body and him slowing down to a snail's pace.

"Oh, Amigo, this fills me with dread. See how fast the current is flowing? No, I just can't do it!" he moans.

"Mouse, Mouse, Mouse, weren't you the one who sailed the seas and survived a shipwreck?" I remind him.

"Sì, Cat, but I was younger and had a life vest," Mouse laments.

"Oh, you silly creature, just climb on my head," laughing I chide him. His fear is something I didn't expect. After all, we have faced coyotes, park rangers, a flood, and more.

"Hey, watch out for the ears!" I bark at him as he pulls himself onto my head. When he is settled, I ease myself down towards the water.

"Ok, Mexico, here we come!" we yell at the top of our lungs.

****

The story continues in book 2, *The Perilous Rescue*. Join our two heroes in the thrilling rescue of Momma Cat, her kittens, and hundreds of other cats captured by the Boogey Man.

****

The Perilous Rescue

Margo Cunningham

****

Chapter 1

Not a Good Beginning

Finally, we are on our way. The joy of looking for momma overwhelms me and I sprint down the river bank. "Oh, no!" In my excitement I have gained too much speed and trip over a rock. The rest of the way down the bank I am flipping head over tail.

"EEEEYOW!" Whump. "YOW!" Whump. "YOW!" Crash. "OOF!"

"Help!" screams Mouse as he is flung from my head.

"Where am I?" I wheeze groaning and lying on my back. Before I can move, I hear a very weird noise.

"I say that was an eight," a very small metallic voice pierces the air.

"No, no, no, that wasn't even a five," chimes another small creaky voice.

"You are both wrong! That was ten," grumpily quips a third strange voice. They begin to argue about the score for my flips.

"Eight!" Rattle, rattle.

"Five!" Scuttle, shake.

"Ten!" Stomp, stomp.

"What are you, guys?" I ask as I gaze upon three of the strangest creatures. Their tails and their whole backside curve up over their heads. There appears to be some sort of weapon on the end of their tails. They are shaking and thrusting it at each other as they circle around me.

****

About the Author

Ms. Cunningham lives in Mount Vernon, WA with her husband, Burt, and is currently down to just one cat and one dog. All of the cat names come from a few of the cats she and her mom have had.

Scooby Doo the guinea pig and Lily the cat still live with the Gomez family in El Paso, TX.

41783290R00033

Made in the USA
San Bernardino, CA
20 November 2016